ROBIN HOOD

A High-Spirited Tale of Adventure

Starring
JIM HENSON'S MUPPETS

Kermit the Frog as Robin Hood
Miss Piggy as Maid Marian
Fozzie Bear as Little John
Floyd as Will Scarlet
Lew Zeeland as Friar Tuck
Bunsen Honeydew as George-a-Green
Beauregard as Much the Miller's Son
Rowlf as Allin-a-Dale
Plus a cast of Muppets™
as bold men and hardy!
The Great Gonzo as
the Sheriff of Nottingham
Sam the Eagle as the Town Judge
Animal as himself

Written by
Jocelyn Stevenson

Designed and Illustrated by
Bruce McNally
For James and Julie

BELLWOOD PUBLIC LIBRARY

© Henson Associates, Inc., 1980. THE MUPPET SHOW, MUPPET, and MUPPET character names
are trademarks of Henson Associates, Inc. A Muppet Press Book produced by Henson Organization
Publishing in association with Random House, Inc. All rights reserved under International and Pan-
American Copyright Conventions. Published in the United States by Random House, Inc., New York,
and simultaneously in Canada by Random House of Canada Limited, Toronto.

Library of Congress Cataloging in Publication Data: Main entry under title:
Robin Hood, a high-spirited tale of adventure.
SUMMARY: Traditional tales of Robin Hood, Maid Marian, and the merry outlaws, as depicted by
the Muppet characters.
1. Robin Hood—Legends. (1. Robin Hood. 2. Folklore—England) I. Muppet Press II. Robin Hood.
PZ8.1.R55Mu   1980   398.2'2'0941   80-5083
ISBN 0-394-84568-4 (trade); ISBN 0-394-94568-9 (lib. bdg.)
Manufactured in the United States of America
1 2 3 4 5 6 7 8 9 0

Chapter One

Robin Hood, Maid Marian and a merry band of outlaws lived deep in Sherwood Forest, under the greenwood trees. Robin, a bold and chivalrous frog, led his dauntless men on courageous exploits against mean rich villains. The bold-spirited band stole from the rich and gave to the poor folk who lived off the land. And they always answered the call of a damsel in distress.
(Damsel-in-Distress Hot Line, Sherwood 7204)

Though well-loved by the poor people they so often helped, Robin and his men were despised by the rich and powerful. Their arch enemy was Gonzo, the Sheriff of Nottingham—the foulest, basest, most rascally and hook-nosed sheriff ever to live. The Sheriff and his ruthless gang of men lived in an abandoned castle about two leagues from Sherwood Forest.

They spent most of their free time stealing
everything Robin Hood had given to the poor
and returning it to the rich.
And they always sneered
at a damsel in distress.

One day, Will Scarlet had
just about had enough. "Robin,
my man," he said to his
leader, "we've got to do
something about that dude
Gonzo. We can't allow him to
go around messin' with our
good deeds, you dig?
It's not cool."

"NOT COOL! NOT COOL!"
agreed Animal.

"I know," said Robin. "But be of good cheer. I've been thinking about the situation, and I have an idea. We'll meet the scoundrel Gonzo and his men in an archery tournament. If we win, they leave the forest. If they win, we... but they won't win!...er, I hope."

"Excuse me," said the Town Judge, appearing from behind a bush where he'd been hiding. "I couldn't help overhearing. You're going to have an archery tournament?"

"Yes," said Robin Hood, not exactly thrilled to see the Judge. Sam the Eagle was the self-appointed Judge of Nottingham. He thought Robin Hood and his merry band were undignified and weird. "Is that all right with you?" added Robin obligingly.

"Certainly," answered Sam. "But I insist that I judge the contest. My presence will make the occasion an honorable and noble one, since you're all so undignified and weird."

Robin sighed and agreed.

Chapter Two

Robin Hood, Maid Marian, Will Scarlet, Allin-a-Dale and the rest of the band practiced heartily for the big tournament. They shot arrow after arrow, but only Robin, the best archer in all the land, was able to hit the target anywhere near the bull's-eye.

"We definitely need an archer who can shoot straight and true," said Robin. "Or else, we don't stand a chance. I'll go into town and see if I can find someone who's handy with a bow and arrow."

On his way to place an ad with the nearest town crier, Robin came to a very narrow bridge which crossed over a stream. When Robin walked onto the bridge, he was so lost in thought that he didn't notice the banana peel in the middle of his path. Naturally, he slipped on the peel and landed in the water.

Robin sat dazed in the middle of the stream, then slowly stood up. He was wet from head to flipper and covered with mud.

When he wiped the water from his eyes, he saw a friendly looking brown bear wearing a polka dot bow tie come out from behind a tree.

"Are you hurt, good sir?" asked the bear politely, choking back a guffaw.

"No, just wet," answered Robin.

"Well, you have to admit," said the bear as he laughed and wiggled his ears, "that joke is pretty funneee! But I didn't think someone like you would fall for it. Get it? *Fall* for it?" Robin got it, but ignored it. The bear continued. "Yes, I see. Well, let me explain. I put the banana peel there for a bad guy like the Sheriff or the Judge. But, it was still pretty funneee—no offense."

"Yes, well, er…" Robin Hood was at a loss for words. He felt that it was good fortune to meet such a pleasant bear and true. The question was, could the bear shoot an arrow *and* hit the target? "I think your banana peel joke is very funny. Not too original, but funny." Robin paused. "But, what I really want to know is, do you happen to be an archer?"

"Am *I* an archer?" the bear gasped. "Am I…sir, you have come to the right place. I am one of the best archers ever to wear a fake nose."

And he picked up an arrow and his bow, aimed at a walnut on a tree six miles away, let the arrow fly, and hit the walnut dead center.

"Yes," he said, leaning against his bow, "the bear can arch."

"I pray thee, good bear," said Robin, goodly impressed with the bear's shooting and with the squirrel's reflexes, "will you join my merry band of outlaws and help us win the contest against the Sheriff of Nottingham?"

"Merry band of outlaws?" repeated the bear. "Did you say...could you be...is it true that...are you Robin Hood of Sherwood Forest?" The bear romped with excitement.

"Yes," said Robin modestly. "You've heard of me?"

"Heard of you?" said the bear. "Who hasn't heard of you? Why my kid sister Maid Martha has your picture plastered all over the cave. Think of it...*the* Robin Hood."

"Gee..." Robin was a little embarrassed. "Er, will you join the band against the Sheriff?"

"Gladly," said the bear. "Let me pack." And he went behind a tree and reappeared with a small overnight bag.

"By the way," said Robin, "what's your name?"

"Fozzie, with an e," said the bear proudly.

"Fozzie? Fozzie? What kind of name is Fozzie? If you don't mind, I think we'd better change it to Little John. We're in the Middle Ages. People have names like Edward II and Friar Tuck. No one will understand Fozzie."

"Little John it is," said Little John.

Then Robin blew his horn and the rest of the band appeared out of nowhere to escort their leader and their new recruit back to Sherwood Forest.

Chapter Three

The day of the archery tournament came at last. The fair grounds were gaily decorated for the occasion, and the competition was soon under way. Thanks to Little John, the Sheriff and his men were soundly beaten.

The Sheriff was furious, and the Judge thought the entire event was frivolous and degrading. "It was like something out of the Middle Ages," he muttered.

Robin's merry men wasted no time celebrating their valiant victory. They cavorted and frolicked with hey! with ho! with hoy! until Will Scarlet turned to say something to Robin Hood and noticed that the sylvan leader was goodly and missing.

He was gone...goodbye...he'd disappeared into thin air.

Suddenly, two bushes parted to reveal the frantic face of the resident vision of loveliness. "Help! Help!" cried Maid Marian, waving a piece of parchment over her head. "Look, look! It is a note from that creep the Sheriff of Nottingham. He has my Robbie!" Maid Marian showed the rest of the band a short but informative letter:

Dear Merry Band,
Ha! I win! I have
Robin Hood and the Judge. If you
don't leave the forest for good, you will
never see your leader again.
Take that!
Yours faithfully,
Gonzo,
Sheriff of Nottingham
P.S. If you are still here tomorrow morning, I will
KEEP Robin and GIVE BACK
the Judge! Ha! Ha!

"Oh! Oh!" wailed
Maid Marian. "We must
rescue our Robin!"

"Good thinking,"
said Will Scarlet.

"I totally agree," said
one of the more
scientific merry men,
"but how?"

Now, Maid Marian was in truth an extremely glamorous pig who had fallen in love with Robin Hood and had come to live in the Forest to cook and sew for her frog and his merry men. The problem was that she hated living under the greenwood trees, or any trees for that matter.

First of all, she was not particularly interested in the great outdoors. "If you've seen one tree, you've seen them all," she often said. But most of all, she missed the simple comforts of life, such as hair curlers and chocolate bonbons (not to mention electricity and running water). However, at this moment of crisis she surprised everyone by quickly organizing a brilliant campaign to rescue their leader.

"We go to the Sheriff's castle and take him back," she said. Dazzled by her superior mental acuteness, the merry band immediately followed her orders. They picked up their bows, jumped on their horses, and made haste for the Sheriff's castle. They were just about to cross the draw-bridge to enter the vile fortress, when they saw the Sheriff himself mounted on his black steed, surrounded by seven or eight of his most bloodthirsty men.

Gonzo's Castle

"Hey nonny nonny no!" he cried. "I've been expecting you."

"What have you done with my Robbie?" demanded Maid Marian.

"Nothing, m'lady, nothing...yet!" said the odious Sheriff with a nasty giggle. "And I will keep doing nothing to him if, and only if, you leave the forest—all of you—*now!*"

"But, prithee, what if we don't want to?" asked Little John bravely.

"Yeah," said Much the Miller's son in support.

"That's your affair," answered the Sheriff with a wicked gleam on his nose. "But until you all leave the forest, I will not give your precious Robin any food, water, or telephone messages."

"You heartless knave!" cried Maid Marian. "You buzzard-beaked wimp, you..."

"Never mind," interrupted the Sheriff. "Just get out of the forest if you know what's good for you." And he reared his horse and galloped into the castle, pulling up the drawbridge behind him.

Chapter Four

Maid Marian and the now not-so-merry men rode slowly into the forest to figure out what to do.

"You know, I never liked this silly forest anyway," said Maid Marian, trying to be helpful. "Maybe we could find a cute little house somewhere where I could take bubble baths and have a place to plug in my hair dryer. Then Robbie would be set free and we'd all live happily ever after, hmmm?"

× HOME SWEET HOME ×

"But, Maid Marian," said Little John, "Robin loves the forest. He needs room to arch and make merry. He couldn't live in a house."

"So how about in a fish pond with big lily pads?" she asked.

The men sadly shook their heads.

"Well, I tried," sighed Maid Marian. "But no Sheriff is going to kidnap my Robbie and get away with it. Let's find an army and storm the castle!"

Startled once again by Maid Marian's military flair, Robin's men agreed to her latest plan and spread out to recruit an army.

Chapter Five

By sundown, they had mobilized a large and mighty force of…chickens.

"Chickens?!" shrieked Maid Marian. "I ask for an army and you bring me chickens?"

"But stay, fair lady," said Little John. "These are stout-hearted chickens. No chicken chicken here. Get it? *Chicken* chicken…you don't get it. They will cross the road and fight to the finish!!

"You can count on a chicken to be a good egg. A good egg! Chicken...egg...ooohhh, that's funneeee!" And Little John rolled on the ground, laughing.

"I'll show you funnee," said Maid Marian, but she was interrupted by Camilla, the Head Hen.

"Cluck! Cluckcluck!" Camilla ordered. The army of chickens fell into formation.

"Ca-luck!" They drew their swords.

"OH!" gasped Maid Marian. "I see what you mean. Nice little chickens. A wonderful army! Very efficient. Très brave, too. LET'S GO!!"

Little John and his horse went ahead to scout out the castle and lower the drawbridge. The horse spurred Little John on and they arrived at the Sheriff's fortress in good time. The drawbridge was down. "That's funny," said Little John. "It wasn't down before." And as he crossed the drawbridge into the castle, his horse slipped on a banana peel and they both fell into the muddy moat.

"Drats!" yelled Little John. "Somebody stole my best joke!"

Meanwhile, the chickens
and outlaws, led by Maid Marian,
speedily made their way
toward the sinister fortress where
their hero was held prisoner.
They rode quietly, and approached
the castle unnoticed.
The night was very, very dark.
   "I can't see a thing,"
whispered Maid Marian.
   "Me neither,"
said Friar Tuck.
   "Is the bridge down?"
asked Maid Marian.
   "Gee, I hope so, you bet,"
said the Friar.

"Well, here goes nothing," said Maid Marian, and with an ear-shattering "HiiiyaaaaAAAA!!" the chickens and Robin's band rushed over the drawbridge, whooping, clucking, swinging their swords and shooting arrows all over the place.

When they got to the castle door, they were stopped by the Sheriff and his men dressed in second-hand armor. Arrows bounced off their helmets. Swords were powerless against their shields. It looked like the end for Robin's merry men.

But, all of a sudden, something very strange happened to Gonzo. First, he lifted his visor and stared wide-eyed at the chickens. Then he screamed "Wow!," leapt off his horse, clutched his heart and ran towards Camilla and her Hens, waving a white handkerchief. "Chickens!" he cried. "Chickens! My kingdom for your chickens!"

"What?" said Little John, climbing out of the moat.

"Are you crazy?" demanded Maid Marian.

"Crazy?" whispered the stricken Gonzo. "How did you know?"

"Know what?" asked Little John.

"Know I'm crazy about chickens!" and the Sheriff dropped to his knees. "I'll trade you these beautiful chickens for Robin Hood and the Judge and anything else you want. What's a frog, what's an eagle, when I can have chickens?"

"He's got to be kidding," said Maid Marian.
"No," said Little John, "he's just weird.
Sheriffs aren't what they used to be."
"Let's ask the chickies what they think,"
suggested Friar Tuck. He turned to the army.
"Hey little chickies! Wanna stay with the
Sheriff here?"

The chickens huddled for a conference. Camilla clucked something to Friar Tuck. "Hey," the good Friar translated, "they wanna know if there are any stew pots in the castle."

Gonzo was shocked. "No! Not a pot in the place—I promise."

So, the chickens looked at each other and shrugged. Why not?

"Oh thank you!" said the Sheriff, obviously grateful. "I'll take good care of you. And I'll never do a bad deed again as long as I live!"

So the Sheriff led the chickens into the castle and Robin Hood was set free.

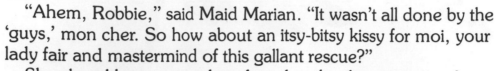

Chapter Six

"Nice work, guys," said Robin to his merry men. "I knew you could do it."

"Ahem, Robbie," said Maid Marian. "It wasn't all done by the 'guys,' mon cher. So how about an itsy-bitsy kissy for moi, your lady fair and mastermind of this gallant rescue?"

She closed her eyes and puckered up her lips, expectantly. Robin Hood leaned towards Maid Marian...then picked up her hand and shook it heartily.

"Thanks a lot, Maid Marian," said Robin. "Now I've got to go rescue the Judge." And he disappeared down into the castle dungeon.

"Chivalry's dead!" Maid Marian screamed after him.

"What d'ya mean, ma'am?" asked Much the Miller's son. "It's just been invented." He then took one look at Maid Marian's face and decided to help Robin in the dungeon.

After much searching, Robin found the Judge locked in a particularly unpleasant cell.

"Oh, please get me out of here," the Judge pleaded. "This is not the place for an honorable eagle, such as myself."

"Okay," said Robin. "I will set you free if you promise never to say that we are undignified and weird again."

"Even though you are?" asked the Judge.

"Yes, even though we...er...Promise never to say it again," said Robin.

The Judge promised, and Robin set him free.

Robin Hood, Maid Marian and the mirthful men returned joyfully to Sherwood Forest. Once back under the greenwood trees, they prepared a huge feast to celebrate their victories. No more evil Sheriff! No more nasty Judge! With hey! With hoy! The revelling and romping went on all night.

Then, just before dawn,
Robin softly blew his horn.
Everyone fell silent,
and he sang this song:

Tirraly terlo
Hey trolly lolly lo!
Not long ago
We smote our foe!
Heigh ho, heigh ho!
Sing yes!   Sing no!
Goodbye, fair friend!
And that's

THE END